39 Kids on the Block

My Sister the Blabbermouth

Look for these and other books in the
39 Kids on the Block series:

39 Kids on the Block

My Sister the Blabbermouth

by Jean Marzollo

Illustrated by Irene Trivas

SCHOLASTIC INC.

New York   Toronto   London   Auckland   Sydney

ISBN 0-590-42728-8

Copyright © 1990 by Jean Marzollo.
All rights reserved. Published by Scholastic Inc.

APPLE PAPERBACKS is a registered trademark of Scholastic Inc.
39 KIDS ON THE BLOCK is a trademark of Scholastic Inc.

12 11 10 9 8 7 6 5 4 3 2   0 1 2 3 4 5/9

Printed in the U.S.A.   40

First Scholastic printing, August 1990

For Elwood and the Earwigs

With special thanks to
Lucinda Lee Katz, Li Wei,
Becky Beane, Kate McMullan,
Bud Spodek, and the children in
Mrs. Liberty's class: David A., J.J.,
Kendall, Karina, Kali, Katie, Conor,
Melissa, Debbie, Ashley, Chris, Rebecca,
David S., Jatinder, Tara, Alicia,
Samantha, Joey, Maria, and Ryan — J.M.

Thirty-nine kids live on Baldwin Street.
They range in age from babies to teenagers.
The main kids in this story are:
Lisa Wu,
Julie Wu,
May-May Wu,
Rusty Morelli,
John Beane,
Michael Finn,
Maria Lopez,
Mary Kate Adams,
Joey Adams,
Donna Finn,
Jane Fox,
Fizz Eddie Fox,
Kimberly Brown.

Chapter 1

"Wake up!" a voice called.

But Lisa Wu didn't want to wake up. She was dreaming her Cinderella dream.

In her dream there were two sisters. The older one was the pretty one. The prince always chose her.

"Wake up!" cried the voice again.

Lisa reached inside her pillowcase. She moved her hand around until she found a small piece of silk.

It was the last piece of her baby blanket. Lisa called it "Quiltie."

Lisa put Quiltie to her cheek and went back to her dream.

"Quiltie, Quiltie, Lisa loves Quiltie," sang the nasty voice.

Lisa shoved Quiltie back into her pillowcase. "Stop saying that!" she cried.

Her dream was gone. Lisa sat up and glared at her sister.

"Get dressed!" yelled Julie. "It's the first day of camp!"

Lisa's sister wore a yellow jersey and yellow shorts. She was brighter than the sun.

Lisa groaned. "I don't want to go to camp."

"Mama! Mama!" yelled Julie, running down the hall. "Lisa doesn't want to go to camp!"

A few seconds later, Mrs. Wu came into the bedroom. She leaned against the doorjamb. Her belly was huge because she was pregnant.

"What's the matter?" she asked Lisa.

"I don't want to go to camp," said Lisa.

"But camp will be fun," said her mother.

"And you have to go. You have to watch Julie."

"Julie is only *one* year younger than I am," said Lisa.

And much better at dodgeball, she wanted to add. But she didn't. It was too embarrassing.

Besides, what did dodgeball matter? The prince never asked if she was good at dodgeball.

Mrs. Wu sat down on Lisa's bed. She rested her hands gently on her belly.

"Lisa my dear," she said. "You are the oldest child in our family. You will make us proud at camp just as you did at school."

Lisa shook her head. It was no use. Her mother would never understand. She had never gone to camp.

Lisa had never gone to camp, either. But she knew what camp would be like. Dodgeball all day long.

Lisa couldn't throw. And she couldn't dodge. Kids would hate her at camp. They would pick her last for their teams.

Mrs. Wu told Lisa to get dressed. Then she left the room.

Lisa put on a gray jersey and gray shorts. They were perfect. Julie looked like the sun. And Lisa looked like a rain cloud.

Rain Cloud and Sunshine looked out the window.

A big blue circle had been painted on the street. Just the right size for dodgeball.

The day before, Lisa had watched Mrs. Morelli and Rusty paint it.

Rusty was Lisa's friend. Mrs. Morelli was Rusty's grandmother. She was also the camp director.

Lisa put on her socks and remembered how the camp idea started.

On the last day of school Mrs. Morelli had picked Rusty up. "What are you going to do this summer?" she asked him.

"Nothing," said Rusty.

"What are *you* going to do?" she asked Lisa.

"Nothing," said Lisa.

All the other kids told Mrs. Morelli the same thing.

"But doing nothing is a drag," she said. "Let's have a day camp on Baldwin Street."

Baldwin Street was the name of their block.

"We'll invite all thirty-nine kids who live here," said Mrs. Morelli.

And so she had. Of course, some kids were too little to join. But many others signed up.

And now the first day of camp had arrived.

"Look!" cried Julie at the window. "The counselors are there!"

Lisa looked out of the window again. She saw Kimberly and Fizz Eddie standing in the blue circle. They were in junior high.

Fizz Eddie got his nickname because he was so good at phys ed. Lisa knew he wouldn't like her at camp. He would get mad at her every time she missed the ball.

"Kimberly has a side ponytail," said Julie.

Julie pulled out her barrette. She brushed her hair to the side. She made a side ponytail like Kimberly's. It looked sort of cute.

Lisa pulled her hair into a side ponytail, too.

"Your hair is too short," said Julie. "Your ponytail looks like a paintbrush."

"Oh yeah? Well, yours looks like a broom," said Lisa.

"Mama!" cried Julie. "Lisa said — "

Lisa grabbed her sister's arm. "Stop telling Mama on me," she said. "And don't be a tattletale at camp. Okay? Kimberly hates tattletales. Fizz Eddie hates tattletales. And I hate tattletales. You heard what Mama said. I'm in charge of you."

Just then, May-May ran into the room. There were no brothers in the Wu family. Just three sisters. May-May was the baby. She was still in diapers.

May-May hid behind Lisa.

"Where's May-May?" asked Mrs. Wu. She came in the room again. This time she was waving a T-shirt in her hands. She was pretending not to see May-May.

"I have no idea," said Lisa. Lisa looked all around. She was pretending, too.

May-May squealed like a happy little pig. Lisa pounced on her little sister and hugged her. She put the T-shirt on her in two seconds.

May-May buried her head in Lisa's neck. "Ma-ma," she said.

"I'm not your mama," said Lisa with a laugh. "I'm your big sister."

"Ma-ma," insisted May-May.

Lisa rocked her back and forth. She sort of felt like a mother.

All of a sudden, Julie took out her barrette and threw it on the floor. "I hate my hair!" she cried. "Lisa said it looks like a broom! I'm not going to camp!"

"Calm down," said Mrs. Wu.

Julie was snuffling hard and shaking her shoulders up and down.

Lisa was sure her sister was faking. But she didn't dare say that.

Julie stuck out her lower lip and looked up at her mother. "Can I stay home with May-May? Please, please, please?"

Lisa couldn't believe it. She looked at her mother sternly. When it came to Julie, her mother could be very wishy-washy.

"Well, I don't know," said Mrs. Wu.

Don't let Julie get away with this! Lisa wanted to scream. But she kept quiet. She couldn't be rude to her mother.

Mrs. Wu put her arm around Julie. "You can stay home just for today," she said. "You and May-May can help me make dumplings."

Lisa was furious. After all, she was the one who really wanted to stay home. So she said loud and clear, "I'll stay home, too, and help."

"Oh no," said her mother. "You're the oldest. Go to camp and make us proud. We will watch you from the window."

"But that's not fair!" shouted Lisa. "You let Julie do whatever she wants!"

As soon as she yelled this, Lisa felt terrible. She was never supposed to shout at her mother.

Thank goodness her father was working at the computer factory. If he had been home, he would have been very angry.

Lisa put her arms around her mother. "I'm sorry," she said. And she meant it.

Lisa gave her mother a quick kiss on the cheek. "I'm going to camp now. I'll make you proud. Good-bye."

"Good-bye," said her mother. She kissed Lisa's forehead. "Have fun. We'll watch you from the window."

Lisa ran out of the apartment and ran down the stairs. Then she heard footsteps behind her.

Guess who it was.

Julie.

The bright yellow sun.

"Wait for me!" she beamed. "I was only kidding! Did I fool you?"

"Not a bit," said Lisa with a fake smile.

Chapter 2

"Good morning," said Uncle Pete. He was sweeping the sidewalk in front of the restaurant.

"Good morning, Uncle," said Lisa. She gave her uncle a little bow.

"We're going to camp," said Julie. She also bowed. "Lisa is afraid, but I'm not."

Lisa grabbed her sister's hand and squeezed it. "What did I tell you about being a tattletale?"

"Ouch!" said Julie. "Stop that!"

"Lisa, please," said Uncle Pete. "Let go of your sister."

"I have to hold her hand," said Lisa. "I'm older."

Uncle Pete nodded. "I see," he said. He looked at Lisa sadly. Even though it was morning, he looked tired.

Lisa wished her uncle were happier.

Until last year he had lived in Chinatown in New York City. Then his wife died. After that, he had moved to Appleville to be near the Wu's.

Uncle Pete had bought the only restaurant on the block. He had turned it into a Chinese restaurant.

Uncle Pete served the best Chinese food for miles around. But most people on Baldwin Street had never eaten Chinese food. They didn't know how good it was. So they didn't come to Uncle Pete's restaurant.

Lisa let go of Julie and gave her uncle a hug. She wished she could find a way to bring him more customers.

"Make us proud at camp," said Uncle Pete.

"I will," said Lisa.

Rain Cloud took Sunshine's hand — nicely this time. They walked over to join the other campers.

Lisa knew her uncle, her mother, and her baby sister were watching her. In a way, she did feel proud.

Mary Kate and John were standing around the blue circle. They were Lisa's friends.

Lisa said hi.

Julie said hi, too.

"You don't have to stay with me," whispered Lisa.

But Julie stuck to Lisa like glue.

Mary Kate and John were trying to sing along with Mrs. Morelli.

Mrs. Morelli was playing an old, beat-up guitar. She was wearing her usual outfit. Paint-covered overalls, an L.A. Dodgers shirt, and an L.A. cap.

Lisa sang, too.

So did Julie.

The song was "I've Been Working on the Railroad."

Mrs. Morelli put down the guitar and grinned. "Ready for camp?" she asked.

"I am," said Julie. "But Lisa didn't want . . . "

Lisa grabbed Julie's hand.

"Excuse us for a minute," she said to Mrs. Morelli.

Lisa yanked Julie off to the side. "What were you going to say about me?" she asked.

"Nothing," said Julie.

Lisa narrowed her eyes. "I'm warning you," she said. "Don't say one word about me! You hear?"

Julie stuck out her lower lip. "I'm sorry," she said. She looked as if she were going to cry. This time for real.

Lisa glanced up at the window. Her mother and May-May were waving.

"All right," said Lisa. "Now turn around and wave to Mama. And smile."

For once, Julie did as she was told.

Fizz Eddie asked the campers to sit around the big blue circle. Lisa sat between Mary Kate and Michael.

"Go sit with your own friends," she told Julie.

"I want to sit with you," said Julie.

"There isn't any room," said Lisa.

Julie thought about that. Then she bent down and sang something to Lisa. "Quiltie, Quiltie."

Lisa was horrified. She yanked her sister into her lap. "Don't you dare tell anyone about Quiltie!" she hissed.

"I won't," said Julie.

Julie sat very still in Lisa's lap. She even put her head back on Lisa's shoulder.

Like a great big heavy baby.

This is going to be a rough summer, thought Lisa.

"We have twenty-eight campers," said

Mrs. Morelli. "That's great! And thanks to John Beane's mother, there will be no traffic on the block."

John's mother was a police officer. Sergeant Beane had asked the police department to keep cars off the street during camp hours.

John looked very proud. And not just of his mother. His grandfather was one of the counselors. Mr. Beane was a Sioux Indian and an author. He had come to Author's Tea at school.

Michael Finn looked proud, too. His sister Donna was a counselor.

Lisa wished she had an older sister, instead of a little brat like Julie.

"The first thing we need is a camp name," said Mrs. Morelli. "Something like the Appleville Camp. But that's too boring. We need an exciting name."

Lisa wondered what Mrs. Morelli meant by "exciting."

Mrs. Morelli was a painter. Her pictures were very unusual. No one could tell what they were.

Maybe to her "exciting" means strange, thought Lisa.

"May I make a suggestion?" asked Mrs. Morelli. "Since this camp was my idea, let's call it the L.A. Dodgers Day Camp."

That's pretty strange, thought Lisa.

"Raise your hand if you like the name," said Mrs. Morelli. "Be honest."

Only Mr. Beane raised his hand.

Michael Finn spoke up. "Mrs. Morelli," he said. "I know you're homesick for California. But this is New Jersey. We like the Mets. So how about the Mets Day Camp?"

"Yankees Day Camp!" cried Jane.

"Mets!" yelled Mary Kate.

"Yankees!" shouted Fizz Eddie.

"Dodgers!" shouted Mr. Beane. He was loudest of all.

Mrs. Morelli laughed. She took off her

baseball cap and shook her hair. She looked pretty when she did that.

Lisa had never thought of Mrs. Morelli as pretty before.

"I loved the Dodgers when they lived in Brooklyn," said Mr. Beane.

"The Dodgers never lived in Brooklyn!" said Michael. He laughed to show that nobody could fool him. After all, he was the smartest kid at school.

"They did so," said Mr. Beane. "They were named the Dodgers because they had to dodge the old Brooklyn trolley cars."

"I have an idea for a name," said Maria. "How about The Grandparents Camp? We can call Mr. Beane 'Grandpa.' And we can call Mrs. Morelli 'Grandma.' "

Mrs. Morelli wrinkled her nose. "Being called Grandma by Rusty is fine," she said. "But being called Grandma by everyone will make me feel too old."

"Me, too," said Mr. Beane.

"Okay," said Fizz Eddie. "Any other ideas?" He laughed.

A strange idea popped into Lisa's head. She wasn't sure anyone else would like it.

I'll try it out on Julie first, she thought.

"How about this?" she whispered to her sister. "The Trolley Car Camp."

Julie raised her hand. "How about the Trolley Car Camp?" she said.

Fizz Eddie laughed. "Who votes yes for the Trolley Car Camp?"

Hands flew into the air. Even Lisa's.

Well, what was she supposed to do? Vote against her own idea?

But inside she was burning. "That was my idea!" she said to Julie.

"That was Lisa's idea," said Julie.

But everyone was talking. So no one heard her.

It's going to be a very, VERY rough summer, thought Lisa.

Mrs. Morelli blew a whistle.

The campers grew quiet.

"That's the Trolley Car Whistle," said Mrs. Morelli. "When you hear it, pipe down. Every morning Trolley Car Camp will start with Circle Time. After Circle Time we'll have Practice Time. After Practice Time, we'll do the usual camp activities. You know — games, sports, crafts, and music."

The minute Lisa heard *sports,* she felt sick. But Practice Time sounded even worse. The only thing worse than playing dodge-ball was practicing it.

"What's Practice Time?" she asked.

"See if you can figure it out," said Mrs. Morelli. "Listen."

The campers listened as the counselors gave them hints.

Kimberly spoke first. "All my life," she said, "I have wanted to learn how to do a cartwheel. Is there anyone who can teach me?"

"I can," said Fizz Eddie.

Kimberly twirled her ponytail in her fingers and smiled at him.

"All my life," said Fizz Eddie, "I have wanted to learn how to juggle. Is there anyone who can teach me?"

"I used to be able to juggle," said Mr. Beane. "I'd be glad to teach you."

Mr. Beane smiled at Mrs. Morelli. "You know what I'd like?" he said. "I'd like to have you teach me how to play the guitar."

"No problem!" said Mrs. Morelli. She looked around at the kids. "Have you figured out what Practice Time is?"

"We're going to watch you learn stuff," said Michael.

"Close but no cigar," said Mrs. Morelli.

"We're going to learn things and teach things, too," said Mary Kate.

"Right!" said Mrs. Morelli. "And the last day of camp could be called Trolley Car Day. We could make a big Trolley Car Stage. And we could take turns performing on it. We could show each other what we've learned. Like a talent show!"

Mrs. Morelli was getting very excited.

"And then," she said, "we'll have a big celebration. I don't know what kind yet. Maybe it will be a surprise."

"Can we suggest ideas for the surprise?" said Michael.

"Of course," said Mrs. Morelli. "That's a great suggestion. But only tell your ideas to me, so they will stay secret. And make sure your ideas are exciting. We could give a prize to the camper with the best idea."

Maybe Lisa could think of another unusual idea. But when she did, she wouldn't try it out first on Julie.

"Now for your homework," said Mrs. Morelli. "Tonight you must think of something to learn at camp. And something to teach."

"I already know what I want to learn," said Mary Kate. "To ride a two-wheel bike. But how can I do that on the Trolley Car Stage?"

"You can ride around it," said Mr. Beane.

"I can teach someone how to say the alphabet backwards," said John. "Z, Y, X, W, V, U, T, S. . . . "

"Teach me!" said Michael.

"Okay," said John. "R, Q, P, O, N, M . . . " He could say it so fast!

Everyone was laughing except Lisa. She loved school homework. But camp homework was different.

What did she want to learn?

She *should* want to learn how to play dodgeball better. She didn't like dodgeball.

What she really wanted to learn was how to whistle. All the other kids her age could whistle.

But it would be embarrassing for Lisa to admit she couldn't whistle.

That was Problem Number One.

Problem Number Two was finding something to teach.

At school Lisa was the best at writing and spelling. But who would want to learn that at camp?

Chapter 3

Lisa cut May-May's dumplings into little bits.

May-May picked them up with her fingers. Some she put in her mouth. Some she put on her cheeks. Lisa tried not to laugh.

"I'm going to learn ballet," said Julie. "Maria Lopez is going to teach me."

"What are you going to teach?" Mr. Wu asked Julie. He was home for supper. He was still dressed in his office clothes — a white shirt and tie.

"How to play dodgeball," said Julie. "We played at camp this afternoon. Lisa was the first one out. I was the last."

"Oh, shut up," said Lisa.

"Lisa! Please be nice to your sister," said Mr. Wu.

"Why don't you tell her to be nice to me?" asked Lisa.

"Don't be fresh," said her father. "You are the oldest. You have to set a good example."

Lisa looked down. There were dumplings on the floor around May-May. She picked them up with a napkin.

Just once, she thought, I'd like to be the baby in the family.

"What about you, Lisa?" said Mrs. Wu. "What are you going to learn at camp?"

Lisa turned to Julie. "You promise you won't tell if I say?"

Julie crossed her heart. "I promise," she said.

"I want to learn to whistle," said Lisa.

"I could teach you." Then Julie whistled "Twinkle, Twinkle, Little Star." The whole thing. From beginning to end. Perfectly.

Did anyone tell Julie to stop?

No.

Lisa wanted to push a dumpling between Julie's lips. But of course she didn't.

She had to set a good example.

That night, Lisa was too upset to sleep.

She sat up in bed and put on the light.

Good, she thought. Julie didn't wake up.

Lisa reached for a clean white pad. She wrote down three things she could teach.

> How to make dumplings.
> How to print neatly.
> How to spell.

It was not a long list.

And not an exciting one.

Lisa sighed and turned the page. She wrote down ideas for the surprise celebration on Trolley Car Day.

A circus.

A camp fire.

A magic show.

This list was better. It would be fun to get the prize for the best idea.

The next morning Mrs. Morelli was playing "I've Been Working on the Railroad" again.

Lisa sat down next to her.

Julie sat down next to Lisa.

"Don't cling!" whispered Lisa. "Go sit with your friends!"

"Quiltie, Quilt — "

"Quiet!" said Lisa. She moved over so her sister had to sit on the ground. Then she gave her sister the meanest look she could.

"I'm cold," said Julie. She huddled close to Lisa.

Lisa looked up at her window. Her mother was watching. Lisa made herself smile and wave back.

Fizz Eddie started Circle Time. "What do you want to learn?" he asked each camper.

One by one, the campers signed up.

Soon it was Lisa's turn.

Lisa was too embarrassed to say "whistling." And she didn't want to say "dodgeball" because she didn't want Julie to be her teacher. So she didn't say anything.

"Lisa?" asked Fizz Eddie.

Lisa just couldn't answer.

"She wants to learn how to whistle," said Julie.

"Be quiet!" said Lisa.

But it was too late. Every camper who could whistle was now whistling.

Lisa couldn't look at them. Going to camp with a blabbermouth sister was the worst thing in the world.

At school, she and Julie were in separate grades. But here at camp they were together all day long.

Lisa blinked to hold back tears.

Then someone spoke to her.

It was Mrs. Morelli. "Lisa, you're just like me," she said. "I couldn't whistle until I was ten."

Lisa blinked again.

Mrs. Morelli had a shawl around her shoulders. It was black with red flowers and gold fringe. The morning sun was shining on her face. And she was smiling her pretty smile at Lisa.

"So what is it going to be?" asked Kimberly.

"Whistling," said Lisa, very softly.

"Who can teach whistling?" asked Fizz Eddie.

Lots of hands went up. And the whistling started up again, too.

Fizz Eddie picked Rusty. Then he said, "Lisa, what can you teach?"

She shrugged and said, "Spelling?"

"If I wasn't learning to juggle, you could teach me," said Fizz Eddie. "I can't spell for beans."

But no one else seemed interested in spelling.

"Tell you what," said Fizz Eddie. "Can you write?"

"She's one of the best in our grade," said Mary Kate.

"Great," said Fizz Eddie. "Because Joey wants someone to write down his stories about space creatures. Think you can do that?"

"Sure!" said Lisa. She looked over at Joey. He was sitting on his sister Mary Kate's lap. Lisa wondered if they ever fought at home.

Joey had his space blanket with him. He wore it to camp everyday like a cape. Maybe someday Joey would only have a piece of it hidden in his pillow.

Writing down Joey's stories would be a breeze.

"Okay, here's the list," said Fizz Eddie. He held it up for all to see. "Those whose

names are on the left will be teachers today. Tomorrow you'll be students."

Kids stood up and paired off.

Joey ran over to Lisa. She picked him up. He was much heavier than May-May. So she put him back down again.

Mr. Beane came over to Mrs. Morelli.

He gave her a big smile. And Mrs. Morelli gave him a big smile back.

"When do my lessons start?" he asked her.

"Right now," she said. Mrs. Morelli picked up her guitar. "Time to go to work, George."

"Who's George?" asked Lisa.

"George is the name of her guitar," explained Mr. Beane. "You ever hear of B.B. King? He calls his guitar Lucille. He's my favorite singer."

"He's my favorite singer, too!" said Mrs. Morelli. "Isn't that amazing?"

Mrs. Morelli smiled her pretty smile again at Mr. Beane.

Mr. Beane smiled back and laughed. And laughed and laughed.

Mrs. Morelli kept grinning back at him.

Something strange and exciting is going on, thought Lisa.

Chapter 4

"Once upon a time there was a big space alien," Joey said. "The alien flew through the sky and crashed into a satellite. The satellite broke. All the people inside fell out."

Lisa stopped writing for a minute. "What kind of people?" she asked.

"Crayon people," said Joey. "There is a red king. And a green queen. You want me to draw a picture of them?"

Lisa watched Joey color. In the background she could hear Mrs. Morelli playing "I've Been Working on the Railroad" again.

She and Mr. Beane were singing it. Every so often, they would stop and laugh.

Then Mr. Beane played the song alone. Very, very slowly.

Mrs. Morelli came over and looked at Joey's drawing. It was a big scribbly mess. You couldn't tell it was a picture of a king and a queen.

"Sensational!" said Mrs. Morelli. "You're so free, Joey! I could learn from you."

Lisa didn't know if Mrs. Morelli was kidding or not.

One of Mrs. Morelli's paintings was hanging at school. It did look like a kid's picture.

Michael ran over. "Mrs. Morelli!" he shouted. "I have an idea for Trolley Car Day!"

"What is it?" she asked.

"A circus!" he said.

Mrs. Morelli didn't look too excited. "I'm not too crazy about circuses," she said. "But we'll see."

Lisa had a strong feeling that there would not be a circus on Trolley Car Day. Now she only had two good ideas left: a camp fire and a magic show.

"Lick your lips," said Rusty. "Not too much. Like this."

Lisa licked her lips.

"Now put your lips like this," said Rusty. He made his mouth into a little circle.

So did Lisa.

"Now blow," said Rusty. A sweet sound came out of his lips.

A puff of air came out of Lisa's.

"You're blowing too hard," said Rusty.

Lisa tried again — softly.

"Or maybe not hard enough," said Rusty.

Lisa tried again with more force. She sounded as if she were trying to blow out a candle.

All air and no music.

And it was the end of the third week of camp.

The cool weather had gone. And a heat wave had arrived.

Lisa was hot and mad.

She would never learn to whistle. On Trolley Car Day she would make a fool out of herself.

"Don't be discouraged," said Fizz Eddie. "I can't juggle yet, either."

"And I can't ride a bike," said Mary Kate. She pointed to the Band-Aids on her knees.

"I can say the alphabet backwards," said Michael. "Listen. Z, Y, X, W, V, U, T. . . ."

"Okay, okay," said Rusty. "We've heard you a million times. Come on, Lisa. Let's get back to work. Put your lips like this."

Lisa copied him exactly.

But once again, she couldn't make a whistling sound.

Mrs. Morelli came over and watched. "Learning to whistle was harder for me than learning to paint," she said.

Lisa stopped trying for a moment. "I have an idea for Trolley Car Day," she said.

"What is it?" asked Mrs. Morelli.

"A camp fire," said Lisa.

"I don't think the fire department would let us have one," said Mrs. Morelli. "But I can always ask."

Lisa only had one good idea left. She wanted to think of more. But she was too busy trying to whistle.

Chapter 5

Every night Julie showed her parents what she had learned.

"This is position one," she said.

Her mother and father clapped. So did May-May.

Lisa fanned herself with a homemade fan.

"This is position two," said Julie.

More clapping.

When Julie was done, she would ask, "Can you whistle yet, Lisa?"

Every night Lisa would have to say no.

Then Julie would whistle "Twinkle, Twinkle, Little Star."

One very hot night in August, Lisa went over to her mother. "Can I go down to see Uncle Pete?" she asked.

Her mother said yes. She liked to have Lisa visit Uncle Pete to cheer him up.

Lisa ran down the stairs. She was sweating. But when she opened the door to Uncle Pete's, cool air hit her face. Uncle Pete's was air-conditioned.

Lisa felt better already.

She had a favorite spot at the bar behind a big palm tree. There, she could watch the bar TV. Customers didn't notice her.

Uncle Pete wasn't around. But Lisa knew he would soon come over. He would bring her a dish of crispy noodles and a glass of juice.

As she waited, Lisa ate some of the bar fruit. Two orange slices and a cherry.

A *Lassie* rerun was playing. Even though the sound was off, Lisa could follow the story.

The mother on *Lassie* always wore

dresses and high heels. There was only one child in her family.

A boy.

Lisa wondered if her mother wanted a boy baby.

She thought about that for a while.

And then she thought about her third idea for Trolley Car Day.

A magic show.

She was sure Mrs. Morelli would love that idea.

But what if she didn't? Lisa really wanted to win the prize for the best idea.

Suddenly, Lisa heard two familiar voices behind her. They were coming from a booth.

The voices belonged to Mrs. Morelli and Mr. Beane.

Great! thought Lisa. I can tell them about the magic show.

But something told Lisa not to turn around.

"Sidney," she heard Mrs. Morelli say. "What's the matter with you tonight?"

Lisa remembered from the Author's Tea that Sidney was Mr. Beane's first name.

"I'm worried," said Mr. Beane. "Maybe we shouldn't get married."

Married? thought Lisa.

She couldn't believe what she was hearing.

"Why not?" asked Mrs. Morelli.

"I'm afraid," said Mr. Beane. "I think I'm too old for change."

"But you only have to move across the street," said Mrs. Morelli. "There's plenty of room. Rusty's parents said it would be fine."

Rusty's parents were away for a year. They were studying trees in Brazil. Lisa wondered if Rusty knew his grandmother wanted to marry Mr. Beane.

She took a deep breath. And held it.

Without thinking Lisa formed her lips

into a circle. It was as if she were saying to herself, "Oooh."

Oooh, I don't believe what I'm hearing.

Oooh, I shouldn't be listening.

Oooh, I wish John and Rusty were here.

"What will John and Rusty think?" asked Mr. Beane. "They'll be so surprised. No one knows about us."

Except me, thought Lisa.

"What are you really saying, Sidney?" said Mrs. Morelli. Her voice sounded nice. But very sad, too. "Don't you love me anymore?"

It was a very important question.

But Lisa had held her breath too long. She had to let it out. And when she did, she whistled.

For the very first time.

She was so surprised that she forgot to listen for Mr. Beane's answer. She even forgot about the question.

Very carefully, Lisa tried to whistle

again. She took a deep breath. Held it. Made her mouth go "Oooh." And whistled.

She did it!

Again!

And again and again!

"Are you okay?" asked Uncle Pete.

Lisa jumped.

"I'm fine," she said.

Her uncle looked very tired. But he was glad to see Lisa. "You want crispy chicken?" he asked.

"No, no, that's okay," said Lisa.

"You want ice cream?"

"No, no, I'm fine. Listen!"

Lisa whistled perfectly.

She could only whistle one note. But it was beautiful.

Uncle Pete was very proud. "I'll bring you a fortune cookie," he said.

He left to go to the kitchen.

Suddenly Lisa remembered Mrs. Morelli and Mr. Beane. They were in love and going to get married! Mr. Beane was going to move into Rusty's house! And she was the only one who knew about it!

Lisa listened.

There were no more voices.

Slowly Lisa turned around. She peeked through the branches of the palm tree.

Mrs. Morelli and Mr. Beane had left.

Uncle Pete brought Lisa her fortune cookie.

Lisa opened it.

YOU WILL MAKE THREE PEOPLE VERY HAPPY THIS MONTH it said.

Lisa hoped that two of the people were Mrs. Morelli and Mr. Beane.

But who would the third person be?

Lisa looked at her tired uncle. Suddenly her heart leaped. The third person could be Uncle Pete!

He could have the wedding reception in his restaurant! This way he would get lots of customers. And Mrs. Morelli and Mr. Beane would have a wonderful party.

Lisa was filled with ideas. Uncle Pete

would make delicious food. And she would make all the decorations.

But she would need help. Who could help her?

Rusty and John, of course! Because it was their grandparents who were getting married.

But was it all right to tell them about the wedding?

After all, it was a secret. And Lisa wasn't supposed to know it.

Lisa had never been a tattletale in her whole life. And she didn't want to start being one now.

So, as she ate her fortune cookie, Lisa thought of a way for Rusty and John to find out the secret. And for someone else to be the tattletale.

Lisa went upstairs to her apartment. Her mother was reading. Her father was using the computer. Julie was watching TV.

"Hi," said Lisa.

"Hi," they said. They couldn't tell she had a secret.

Good. Lisa had to be cool if her plan was to work.

Lisa walked down the hall.

May-May was in her crib in her parents' room. She wasn't asleep yet.

Perfect.

Lisa knelt down next to the crib. She put her face up to the slats.

"Mrs. Morelli and Mr. Beane are in love," she told May-May.

"What are you saying?" asked Julie. Her sister had snuck up behind her. Just as Lisa knew she would.

"Nothing," said Lisa.

"Something about Mrs. Morelli and Mr. Beane," said Julie.

"Don't be silly," said Lisa. "Why would I talk about them?"

"Mama, Lisa's teasing me," whined Julie. She ran down the hall to the living room.

Lisa smiled. She went to her room and changed into her pajamas. She got into bed and started writing on a pad.

M.M. + S.B. she wrote. M.M. stood for Mary Morelli. S.B. stood for Sidney Beane.

Julie came in and got into her pajamas. She looked at the pad.

"What do those letters mean?" she asked.

"Nothing," said Lisa. She drew a big heart. Inside she wrote *M.M. LOVES S.B.*

"I'll tell Mama," said Julie. "You're teasing me again."

"No, I'm not," said Lisa.

But she was. It was all part of the plan.

"I'll tell your friends about Quiltie," said Julie.

But Lisa wasn't worried. She gave her sister a nice, warm, sisterly smile.

Then she drew another heart with a fancy border.

Julie pretended not to look.

But Lisa knew her sister was burning with curiosity.

* * *

"Good night, girls," said Mr. Wu. He gave each girl a kiss and turned off the light.

Lisa could hear Julie breathing. Not the slow way she breathed when she was asleep. The fast way when she was wide awake and mad.

Lisa reached into her pillow. "Quiltie," she said, just loud enough for Julie to hear. "Guess what?"

Lisa heard Julie hold her breath.

"Mrs. Morelli and Mr. Beane are in love," said Lisa. "They are going to get married. And they're going to have the reception in Uncle Pete's Restaurant. We're the only ones who know. Rusty and John don't even know. So don't tell them. Okay, Quiltie?"

Chapter 6

The next day at Circle Time, Julie sat next to Rusty. She whispered something in his ear.

Rusty's eyes opened wide. He stared at his grandmother.

Lisa couldn't stop smiling.

Fizz Eddie asked her, "What are you smiling at?"

"I learned to whistle," she said.

"Great!" said Kimberly. "Let's hear it."

Lisa whistled her one-note whistle.

But that wasn't really why she was smiling. She was really smiling because Julie was now sitting next to John. She whispered something in his ear, too.

John's eyes opened wide. He stared at his grandfather.

Mr. Beane was playing his guitar very softly. He watched the strings as he played. He looked upset.

He didn't look at Mrs. Morelli. And Mrs. Morelli didn't look at him.

Lisa was confused. Why weren't Mrs. Morelli and Mr. Beane smiling and laughing as usual?

Then Lisa remembered the big question. It had happened just before she whistled.

Mrs. Morelli had asked Mr. Beane if he still loved her.

Lisa hadn't heard the answer. She had been too busy whistling.

What if Mr. Beane had said no?

Then he and Mrs. Morelli would not get married. They would not have a reception at Uncle Pete's.

Lisa looked at Mrs. Morelli. She looked

tired and unhappy. As if she hadn't slept all night.

Circle Time was over. Rusty started talking with John. They did not look happy.

"What's the matter?" Lisa asked them.

John and Rusty looked embarrassed.

Rusty shook his head back and forth. Then finally he said, "Your sister told us a big secret. She told us not to tell anyone else. She said that my grandmother is getting married to Mr. Beane. But how can that be? My grandmother was crying last night."

"I don't understand," said John. "I wasn't that surprised by Julie's secret. My grandfather was always talking about Mrs. Morelli at home. But this morning he was very grumpy. I mentioned her name, and he got mad at me."

Lisa felt terrible. Mrs. Morelli and Mr. Beane had a special secret. Once it was a happy secret. And now it was a sad secret. But to them it was always a secret.

And now because of Lisa, it was being blabbed all over the place.

Lisa saw Julie talking to more kids. They were looking shocked. Kids were staring at Mr. Beane and Mrs. Morelli in amazement.

Julie was a blabbermouth. But Lisa was the biggest blabbermouth of all. Because she had given the secret to Julie. And she had hoped Julie would blab it.

What should I do? she wondered.

Lisa felt like quitting camp and running home. She wanted to get into bed with Quiltie and dream her Cinderella dream.

Tears dripped down Lisa's cheeks. She wiped them away with her hand.

"Lisa, why are YOU crying?" asked Rusty.

Lisa wiped her eyes. "This is all my fault," she said. "I guess I better tell you what happened."

Lisa told Rusty and John the whole story.

At the end, the two boys were silent.

"It's too late to stop Julie," said John.

"I know," said Lisa.

"But the important thing is to know the truth," said Rusty. He turned to John. "Do you think your grandfather still loves my grandmother?" asked Rusty. "Because I think she really loves him."

"I think so," said John. "But Grampa is old-fashioned. I can't picture him getting married again."

The three children looked over at Mr. Beane. He was watching Fizz Eddie juggle. Fizz Eddie was doing fine. But Mr. Beane looked miserable.

"We have to help him," said Rusty.

"My fortune cookie said, 'You will make three people very happy this month,' " said Lisa. She told them about her idea for the wedding reception.

Just then, the children heard the Trolley Car Whistle. They went over to join the other campers around Mrs. Morelli.

"I'm sorry, but I don't feel well," she said. "I have to go home. I have a painting to finish for the museum. If anyone needs me, come to the house."

Mrs. Morelli turned around and walked away. She didn't smile. She didn't wave good-bye.

Joey ran over to Lisa. "Are you ready to do my story?" he asked.

"Sure," said Lisa. But it was the last thing she wanted to do.

"The red king and the green queen are captured by Dracula," he said. "Then Wing Boy comes to the rescue."

Wing Boy was Joey's invention. Wing Boy had wings and was afraid of nothing.

Lisa wondered if Joey had heard about Mrs. Morelli and Mr. Beane. She didn't think so.

Joey drew a picture of Wing Boy fighting Dracula.

As he drew, Lisa remembered how pretty Mrs. Morelli looked when she was happy.

"Let's go show that picture to Mrs. Morelli," said Lisa. "It's the kind she likes best."

Lisa didn't know what she was going to say to Mrs. Morelli. But she knew she had to see her.

Lisa and Joey walked up the path to Rusty's house. They stepped onto the porch. It sounded like an orchestra was playing church music in the house.

Lisa knocked.

And knocked again. She wondered if Mrs. Morelli could hear her over the loud music.

"Come on," she said. Lisa led Joey off the porch. They walked around the side of the house.

There was nobody in the living room.

Or the dining room. But when they got to the kitchen, they saw her.

Mrs. Morelli had her head down on the kitchen table. All the windows were open.

Lisa and Joey could hear her sobbing.

"Mrs. Morelli got a boo-boo?" asked Joey.

Kids, thought Lisa. They don't understand anything.

"Yes," she said. "Let's go get Mr. Beane. Maybe he can fix it."

Lisa and Joey ran back to the street. Mr. Beane was still sitting on the curb. He was still watching Fizz Eddie juggle three balls.

And he still looked miserable.

"Excuse me," said Lisa. "But I thought you should know. Mrs. Morelli is crying in her kitchen."

Mr. Beane stood up. "Fizz Eddie," he said. "I don't feel well, either. I have to go home for a minute. Please watch the campers very carefully."

After Mr. Beane left, Fizz Eddie looked at Lisa. "Do you know what your sister is telling everyone?" he asked.

Lisa nodded.

"What's going on?" asked Fizz Eddie.

Fizz Eddie was almost a grown-up. And he had always been nice to Lisa. He had never made fun of her once during dodgeball games.

Dodgeball. Lisa couldn't believe how much she had worried about it in June.

She wished dodgeball were her only problem now.

She looked closely at Fizz Eddie. Hadn't he said that she should be his spelling teacher? Lisa thought she could tell him the truth.

So she said, "It's all my fault." Then she told Fizz Eddie the whole story.

"What a mess," he said. He turned to John. "Maybe you could talk to your grandfather. Find out if he loves Mrs. Morelli or not."

"I know he does," said John.

"Then tell him he's not too old to get married."

"My grandfather's not going to listen to me," said John.

"I've got an idea," said Lisa. "It's different. But it just might work. Mrs. Morelli loves Joey's crazy stories. So, let's ask her if we can make one into a play to perform on Trolley Car Day. It could be the big surprise. A play by a three-year-old."

Rusty looked confused. "But how will it help her and Mr. Beane?"

"We'll ask your grandmother to play the crayon queen," said Lisa. She turned to John. "And your grandfather to be the crayon king."

"So?" said Fizz Eddie.

"There will be a surprise wedding in the play," said Lisa. "The crayon king and the crayon queen won't know it ahead of time."

"I like that plan," said John. "Because it might give Grampa a hint."

* * *

Mrs. Morelli said yes. Joey's play could be the Trolley Car Day surprise.

"Do I get the prize?" asked Lisa.

"What prize?" said Mrs. Morelli.

"For thinking of the best surprise," said Lisa. "Remember?"

"Okay, yes, sure," said Mrs. Morelli. She didn't sound very excited. But then, she never did anymore.

"Joey wants you to play the queen," said Lisa.

"Okay, if that's what he wants," said Mrs. Morelli.

She looked sad and old. But soon she will get her prince, thought Lisa.

Rusty asked Mr. Beane if he would be the crayon king.

"I guess so," he said.

He and Mrs. Morelli hardly even looked at each other.

But that didn't bother Lisa.

Or Fizz Eddie.

Or Rusty.

Or John.

Their plan was going forward perfectly. One by one they told all the kids. Everyone agreed to help.

Even Julie.

She was friendly to Lisa now. She seemed to like the idea that Lisa, not Julie, had been the biggest blabbermouth.

And one thing Lisa was really glad about. Julie hadn't told anyone about Quiltie.

Lisa and Julie made a gown from an old white sheet.

Rusty and John made crowns from gold paper and glitter.

Mary Kate and Michael made little hats for the flower girls.

Maria and Fizz Eddie made bow ties for the ring bearers.

Chapter 7

It was Trolley Car Day.

Fizz Eddie and Joey led parents to their seats on blankets. Mrs. Wu had a special lawn chair. She was too big to sit on the pavement.

In front was the Trolley Car Stage. It was really just four strong tables pushed together. Some of the campers had decorated it with crepe paper.

Kimberly had made a big sign. It read WELCOME TO TROLLEY CAR DAY.

On the stage sat Mrs. Morelli and Mr. Beane. Mrs. Morelli looked great in her

gown. And Mr. Beane looked handsome in his robe.

But they didn't talk to each other.

A curtain had been strung across the street behind the stage.

Behind the curtain, Lisa, Rusty, and John gathered all of the campers together. They helped them put on their hats and bow ties.

Julie stood next to Lisa. She jumped up and down with excitement.

"What about the talent show?" she asked.

"That will come later," said Fizz Eddie. "After the big surprise."

Fizz Eddie stood in front of the stage. He juggled as he spoke.

"Ladies and gentlemen," he said. "May I present the king and queen of Trolley Car Camp!"

Mrs. Morelli and Mr. Beane stood up

and bowed. They didn't smile. The audience clapped.

Then Fizz Eddie started to sing the wedding song. *Da-da-da-dum. Da-da-da-dum.*

As he sang, he kept juggling.

The flower girls and the ring bearers marched to the music. They stopped in front of the stage.

Everybody had a fist full of confetti. And everybody sang.

Da-da-da-dum. Da-da-da-dum.

Mrs. Morelli looked puzzled.

So did Mr. Beane.

The singing stopped.

Lisa and Joey stepped forward.

"Welcome to Trolley Car Day," said Lisa. "Today we are celebrating many things. All the things we have learned. And all of the things we have taught each other. We are going to show them to you. First is a play by Joey Adams. I helped him write it. Are you ready, Joey?"

Joey nodded. He knew his story by heart. "Once upon a time in the land of crayons there was a king and queen."

Joey looked up at Mrs. Morelli and Mr. Beane.

They smiled at Joey. But not at each other.

"The king and queen were going to get married," said Joey. "But then they had a big fight. The king thought he was too old to get married."

Mr. Beane began to frown.

"Then Wing Boy came. He waved his magic crayon." Joey took out a crayon and waved it. "The king became young as a prince."

A little smile crept across Mrs. Morelli's face.

But Mr. Beane looked grim.

"The king and queen became happy again," said Joey. "So they decided to get married after all."

Mrs. Morelli put her hand over her

mouth. Lisa could see she was trying not to laugh.

Mr. Beane folded his arms across his chest. He was definitely *not* laughing.

Fizz Eddie started to sing the wedding song again. *Da-da-da-dum. Da-da-da-dum.*

"What's going on here?" asked Mr. Beane. He sounded very angry.

Joey looked scared.

Lisa felt she should explain. But she didn't know what to say. She hadn't expected Mr. Beane to get so mad.

She looked at Fizz Eddie. He looked nervous, too.

Julie stepped forward. "Can I tell?" she asked.

"Go ahead," said Lisa. For once, she was glad Julie was a blabbermouth.

Julie walked up on the Trolley Car Stage. She put her hand on Mr. Beane's arm.

"We know that you love Mrs. Morelli," she said. "And that you want to get married.

We also know you think you're too old. But you're not too old. I mean, you're old, but not TOO old."

"Julie! Stop saying those things!" said Mrs. Wu. She rose from her lawn chair and came forward. "Mrs. Morelli and Mr. Beane are grown-ups! Getting married is their business, not yours."

"How did you know about us?" asked Mr. Beane. At last he was beginning to smile, too.

"Lisa heard you talking at Uncle Pete's," said Julie.

Everyone stared at Lisa. Lisa shut her eyes. Her face was hot with shame. The worst thing she could do was to embarrass her parents. And she had just done that.

"Lisa!" cried Mrs. Wu. "How could you spy on people like that!"

"Lisa said that Mrs. Morelli was pretty when she was happy," said Julie. "Lisa wanted her to be pretty and happy again.

She thought she would be happy with Mr. Beane as her prince."

"Julie, stop saying those things! You mustn't . . . oh dear!" Mrs. Wu put her hand on her belly. "Oh dear," she said. "Oh dear!"

Mr. Wu ran forward. "Is it starting?" he asked.

"It's starting," she said.

And so the first Trolley Car Day ended with a surprise nobody had expected. Not even Lisa.

Justin Wu was born at the Appleville Hospital. Now there were 40 kids who lived on the block.

That evening Mrs. Morelli and Mr. Beane came to the hospital to visit.

Lisa and Julie sat with them in the waiting room. Once upon a time, they had been Rain Cloud and Sunshine. Now they were the Sunshine Twins.

"Did you notice?" Lisa asked Julie afterwards.

"Yes," said Julie. "They were holding hands."

Lisa and Julie hugged each other. It wasn't so bad being sisters when you both enjoyed the same things.

Chapter 8

On September first, a real wedding took place in the blue circle. Mrs. Morelli wore her queen's gown. Mr. Beane wore a suit.

Justin Wu wore brand-new baby clothes.

All the campers were flower girls and ring bearers again. As they sat around the circle, they sang, "I've Been Working on the Railroad."

That was Mrs. Morelli's idea. She said she wanted camp songs at her wedding.

A Sioux Episcopal priest performed the wedding ceremony.

He asked Lisa, John, and Rusty to read an American Indian marriage blessing.

Lisa let Julie stand next to her as she read.

Now you will feel no rain read Lisa. *For each of you will be shelter for the other.*

Now you will feel no cold read John. *For each of you will be warmth to the other.*

Lisa imagined snow falling in the months ahead. She pictured Mr. Beane and Mrs. Morelli sitting in front of the fireplace in Rusty's house.

Go now to your dwelling to enter into the days of your life together read Rusty. *And may your days be good and long upon the earth.*

Mrs. Morelli decided to keep her name. "I'm used to Mary Morelli," she told Lisa. "But you can call me Mrs. Beane, if you want. That's a nice name, too."

Both Mrs. Morelli and Mr. Beane said they didn't want presents that cost money.

For presents, they wanted the talent show. They wanted the campers to show what they'd learned at camp.

So Joey read his play again.

Michael said the alphabet backwards.

Mary Kate rode her bike back and forth.

Julie danced.

And Lisa whistled the wedding march.

The party afterwards took place in Uncle Pete's restaurant. Lisa had helped him make a special wedding cake. On top were pink roses and a white dove.

"For peace," said Mrs. Morelli.

"And beauty," said Mr. Beane.

Uncle Pete was thrilled to see his restaurant filled with people.

He served them a menu that Lisa had chosen. Spareribs, egg rolls, fried dumplings, chicken and broccoli, and, Lisa's favorite, Moo Shu pork.

Lisa and Julie showed everyone how to eat the Moo Shu pork.

First you take a thin pancake and spread

it with special sauce. Next you put meat and vegetables on it. Then you roll the pancake up and eat it.

Eating it took a little practice. Especially for Rusty. He couldn't keep his pancake together.

Everyone at the party said they were going to come back to Uncle Pete's restaurant again.

Mrs. Morelli gave her new husband a painting for a wedding present. Lisa couldn't tell what it was a picture of. But Joey said it was a picture of Wing Boy.

Mr. Beane gave Mrs. Morelli an electric guitar and an amp.

"I always wanted an electric guitar," she said.

"What are you going to name it?" asked Lisa.

"Good question," said Mrs. Morelli. "Any suggestions?"

"Georgette," said Fizz Eddie.

"Not bad," said Mrs. Morelli.

Lisa could tell that she was looking for a more exciting name.

"Apples," said Julie.

"That will make me hungry," said Mrs. Morelli.

A very strange and exciting name.

This time Lisa was pretty sure of herself. She didn't need to try her idea out on anybody.

"The L.A. Dodgers," she said loud and clear.

"Perfect," said Mrs. Morelli.

She plugged "L.A. Dodgers" into the amp and started to play "Take Me Out to the Ball Game." Everyone sang along.

Except for one person.

Lisa Wu.

She was whistling.

Here are some other books about the
39 Kids on the Block.

#1 *The Green Ghost of Appleville*

Poor Rusty Morelli. He just moved into a
haunted house. Should Mary Kate help
him? Or should she just stay away?

#2 *The Best Present Ever*

Mary Kate, Jane, Rusty, and Michael all
want to get the best present ever! So who
will be the luckiest kid on the block?

#3 *Roses Are Pink and You Stink!*

Michael Finn is angry with everyone—
Rusty and Mary Kate and John and even
Mr. Carson. Now he'll get back at them
all!

About the Author

"I like writing about children and their families," says author Jean Marzollo. "Children are never boring. Whenever I get stuck for an idea, I visit a classroom and talk to the kids. They give me millions of ideas and all I have to do is choose the right one.

"I also like writing about schools and neighborhoods, which are like great big families. People who go to school together and live together learn a lot from each other. They learn to respect each other's differences. Some of my best friends today are people I grew up and went to school with.

"I remember everything about elementary school—my teacher's names, the lamp with painted roses on it that we gave the teacher when she got married, who cried and why on the playground, and how to make fish with fingerpaint.

"When I write the stories for *39 Kids on the Block,* I draw on my childhood memories and my experiences in schools today. I also live with my two teenage sons and husband in Cold Spring, New York, a community with strong values and lots of stories."

Jean Marzollo has written many picture books, easy-to-read books, and novels for children. She has also written books about children for parents and teachers and articles in *Parents Magazine.*

About the Illustrator

"Jean Marzollo and I have been the best of friends for more than twenty years and we have also worked together on many books," says illustrator Irene Trivas. "She writes about kids, I draw them.

"Once upon a time we both lived in New York and learned all about living in the city. Then we moved away. I went off to Vermont and had to learn how to live in the country. But the kids we met were the same everywhere: complicated, funny, silly, serious, and more imaginative than any grown-up can ever be."

Irene Trivas has illustrated a number of picture books and easy-to-read books for children. She has also written and illustrated her own book, *Emma's Christmas: An Old Song* (Orchard).

BARNEY

Anthony Holcroft
Illustrated by Mark Wilson

Written by Anthony Holcroft
Illustrated by Mark Wilson
Designed by Peter Shaw

Published by Mimosa Publications Pty Ltd
PO Box 779, Hawthorn 3122, Australia
© 1995 Mimosa Publications Pty Ltd
All rights reserved.

Literacy 2000 is a Trademark registered in the
United States Patent and Trademark Office.

Distributed in the United States of America by
  Rigby
  A Division of Reed Elsevier Inc.
  1000 Hart Road
  Barrington, IL 60010
  800-822-8661

05 04 03 02 01
10 9 8 7 6 5
Printed in China through Bookbuilders

ISBN 0 7327 1571 7

Contents

The Problem with Barney

Pete heard about Barney almost as soon as he arrived on the Tozers' farm. Old Barney had lived all his life in a small hut hidden away in the forest – and he lived there still. As Pete listened, he could see the hut in his imagination: the floor was carpeted with leaves, and vines clung to the crumbling walls. The wind and the rain blew in through empty window frames.

"It's a wonder that the old man doesn't freeze out there," said Pete's uncle, Alan Tozer, who with his wife owned the land where Barney had his hut. "He should be in a home, where he'd have proper care."

But it seemed that Barney needed little more than the land itself could provide. Pete's Aunt Alice said that he knew the secret tracks of hare and rabbit like the lines on his hand, and he could point out plants that would cure you of a cold or the stomachache.

"Who would have thought the old man would live as long as he has?" said Alan Tozer. "You could have fooled me."

It was all of ten years ago that the Tozers had bought the 200 acres of ancient forest. Before that, it was owned by Barney's half-brother, Marsden. It had never been farmed, and the heavily wooded land, with its circle

of swamp, stood out like a ragged hedge from the neat crops and pasture land that surrounded it.

Alan told Pete that he sometimes felt annoyed just to look at it. "Good land going to waste," he grumbled.

But when Alan had first tried to buy the land, Marsden hadn't wanted to sell. "The land's no use to me," he said. "But I have to look after my brother. What are you going to do with that land? Cut down the trees – right? And then my brother, he'll be like a shellfish without his shell."

But Alan had been determined. He raised his offer till it was almost double what the land was worth. In the end, Marsden said he could have it, if he'd just get off his doorstep; but he also made a condition. For as long as Barney was alive, and chose to live on the land, no earth must be turned there, nor a tree felled.

"It's only right to protect my brother," said Marsden. "And I want your promise in writing. But when he dies, or goes away, then you can do what you like with it, Mr. Tozer."

That was ten years ago, and Barney was still going strong, even though he couldn't be a day less than eighty. Once a month, in winter and summer, the old man wheeled his barrow a mile to the store; and then he wheeled it back again, heavy with supplies.

"I'm not a betting woman," said Alice Tozer, "but if Barney doesn't outlive the lot of us, I'll eat my hat."

Now it was the fall, and Pete had come to stay on the farm while his parents were overseas. He was a "loner," or that was the

way Alan put it; a solitary sort of boy who enjoyed going off on his own to explore, rather than riding on tractors or harvesters.

Pete knew the farm fairly well, but he'd never really thought about the forest that lay beyond. Now, more than anything, he wanted to see that mysterious Barney.

That evening, Pete watched from his attic window as the mists rose in the twilight. A sprinkling of stars appeared in the sky, but in the forest no light shone. Pete shivered to think that an old man lived in that darkness, in a tumble-down hut with no windows and no chimney.

He could imagine mist swirling through the empty window frames, and frost slowly covering the bed like a stiff, white blanket.

"But perhaps he doesn't feel the cold," said Pete aloud as he curled himself up in his warm bed, like a hare in its nest of grass.

The First Encounter

In the morning after breakfast, Pete asked his aunt if he could visit Barney.

"I don't think you'll find him," she said. "He's shy as a rabbit with strangers. But you can explore across the river if you like. Be careful crossing the bridge, though. It's very old, and it's probably as slippery as a skating rink. You'll need to wear my boots."

Pete was soon setting out into the fresh, fall morning. Dew glistened on the tall grasses like beads of honey, and in the distance the forest cast a broad, dark shadow on the fields. Above the treetops, a hawk floated in the blue air.

It took Pete longer to reach the river than he'd expected. He'd stopped on the way to pick up some interesting stones and put them in his bag, and now the sun was well up in the sky.

Then suddenly the forest rose in front of him. The trees were older than any he had ever seen before. Light fell between them in dusty shafts, and there was a smell of spice in the air. The river flowed brown and silent.

Pete shivered, watching his breath drift mistily in the cold air. For a moment he wondered whether he should run back to the farmhouse. It was then that he saw the bridge. Not far from where he stood, almost hidden, thin planks spanned the river. They were still white with frost. Leaves were rustling in the wind, as if birds were hidden in the trees. It was a sound that made Pete uneasy. He held his breath as he crossed, and tried not to look down at the river moving stealthily below.

On the other side, a path led to a damp tunnel of trees. He stepped warily, like a cat, through the forest, until he came to the edge of a clearing of tall, feathery grasses.

Standing at the far side was an old hut of crumbling, sun-bleached bricks. A sapling grew through the roof where the chimney should have been; a stone fireplace was outside the hut, and beside it, under a gnarled pear tree, stood a rusty hand-pump.

Pete hesitated. Then he hooked his bag on the pump, and stepped cautiously onto the sagging veranda. Bees swarmed around a crack in the gaping doorway, and there was a warm, stale smell.

In the darkness, something stirred like a bird rustling in a nest. Pete couldn't bring himself to look into the dark room. He leaped lightly off the veranda and ran across the grass and into the forest. He didn't once look behind him until he was across the bridge and safely in his uncle's open fields.

It was not until he was almost home that he remembered the bag. His aunt didn't want him to go back. "You can do without it tonight, and it won't be coming to any harm where it is."

"And there are some jobs to do here this afternoon," his uncle added.

But after breakfast next morning, Pete set off again. Once again he found the clearing. Some rabbit skins hung in the old pear tree. This time Barney was sitting on the edge of the veranda.

"Look what we've got here," he said slowly, pointing at something on a stone and then smiling up at Pete. "He lives under the stones and catches insects with that long tongue of his."

Pete went forward slowly and looked at the lizard.

The old man nodded. "Come along, then," he said softly. Barney opened his hand and the lizard jumped onto his palm and scuttled up his sleeve. Barney chuckled, and Pete saw that he had only two teeth in his mouth; one above and one below. His brown face was deeply lined, as though rain had made furrows in his cheeks. But his eyes were sharp and bright, like a hawk's.

Pete felt a little shy. "I think I'll go now," he said.

Barney nodded. "Don't forget your bag, boy." It was hanging on the pump where he had left it. Pete thanked the old man and hurried home.

It was not until later that he found that there was something new in the bag. "They look delicious," said his aunt. "You've done well to pick such nice fresh ones."

Pete looked too, and saw, to his surprise, beautiful little button mushrooms, with the dew still on them. Barney must have picked them for him this morning.

Barney's Family

It was two days before Pete saw Barney again. He spent a whole day sifting through the ruins of the old flour mill, and most of the next afternoon assembling its treasures in his bedroom: an ancient coin, a bathtub leg, and fragments of colored glass, their edges blunted by time.

That evening, he set out to see Barney. He found him picking pears from the old tree beside the hut. He nodded to Pete and handed him a basket. They picked side by side in silence. The dusky-brown pears were ripe, and slid easily into Pete's hands. On the side of the tree where the sun had been, they were warm to touch, like eggs in a nest. On the other side, they were already cold.

Barney stored them in a barrel of sand for the winter. "No need to starve, boy," he said. "There's enough here for all my family."

"Where is your family, Barney?" asked Pete, puzzled. The old man waved a hand like a wand toward the forest, growing shadowy now in the twilight.

"My family is all around me," he said. "Those big trees are my family, and the birds that make their nests in them and the insects that feed on their bark, and the river, and its fish, and the little springs that keep the forest cool in summer."

"Will you show me your family, Barney?" said Pete.

"All in good time," said Barney, grinning. He reached up into the pear tree and shook a branch. There was an answering flutter from the dark cluster of hens sitting in the branches.

"Time to roost, boy," said Barney. "Get off home now, and in the morning we'll see."

Pete sped like a hare through the trees and back across the bridge. Tiny night moths fluttered up around his feet in the

dusty grass, and behind him the forest blinked suddenly and grew dark.

In bed that night, Pete imagined the old man sleeping with his family all around him in the forest.

The next morning, when he looked out of his window, Pete saw the forest rising out of fields silvered with rain. Undaunted, he buttoned up his jacket, wriggled his feet into two pairs of socks and his boots, and set off.

At the bridge
he paused, and a
moment later he saw the
old man emerge from the forest.
He wore an old shirt tucked into his
loose trousers, and a battered hat. He
looked pleased to see Pete. "To tell you
true, boy," he said, "I didn't think you'd be
coming."

He took Pete along the forest track, showing him the trees and calling each by name. He showed him shrubs, too, and tiny scented herbs flowering under his feet. "This is the pepper-tree," said Barney, as he bent over a small bush with leaves blotched scarlet and black.

He made a clucking noise with his tongue. "Old Barney wants a leaf," he murmured.

Gently he plucked a leaf from the stalk and began chewing it between his two remaining teeth. "Good for the toothache," he grinned. "The trees – they're my family. I know every single one – I know them by sight, and I know them by feel. If I was blind now, I'd smell them out – I'm telling you true, boy. I know every one."

"My uncle says he'd like to cut your trees down," said Pete.

The old man grinned. "Boy," he said softly, "your uncle is a man who thinks too much of money. If he looked and listened he would be dazzled by the land. He would know that the trees are sacred, and he would hear the spirit of the forest."

"Is that what you do, Barney?" asked Pete.

"I hear it, and it hears me," said the old man. "There is a secret place, where the spirit listens and helps me when I am in trouble."

"Can I see the place?" asked Pete. "Please, Barney!"

But the old man shook his head. "First you must learn to know the forest and care for everything that lives there – you must become one of the family. And then you will find a secret place of your own." He patted Pete on the shoulder. "Tomorrow I'll show you some more of my family."

There was a scolding waiting for Pete at the farmhouse. What would his parents say, his uncle wanted to know, when they returned home to find Pete in bed with the flu? But Pete's aunt wasn't concerned. "Don't fuss the boy," she said. "A drop of water never hurt anyone."

"Aunt Alice," asked Pete, when he brought his damp clothes downstairs, "do you and Uncle Alan really need that land?"

"*Need* it?" Alice thought for a moment. "Well, no, I don't suppose we do."

Pete's Secret Place

Luckily the morning was clear and blue when Pete set out. He had taken a picnic lunch, and now the whole day stretched deliciously before him. He found Barney making a pronged spear for catching eels at night.

The old man looked pleased when Pete came close, to watch. "Soon you'll be able to help old Barney hunt," he said.

But Pete was troubled. "How can you kill eels and hares when they're part of your family?"

Barney nodded. "I'll tell you true now," he said. "To hunt when the belly is empty is all right; and the eel sliding along the riverbed is a gift to the hungry belly. So is the hare

leaping through the grass.
One time I could pick off a hare
at a hundred yards – too true I
could. But the eyesight's gone bad this
last summer – it's not like it was. So you be
thankful, boy, for your own sharp eyes; and
just remember always to ask forgiveness for
taking the life of a creature, and give thanks
when your belly's full. It's like when you cut
down a tree, boy."

Pete opened his mouth to ask again about
the secret place where Barney spoke to the
spirit. But the old man shook his head.

"There's plenty of time, boy," he said. "Plenty of time. Why don't you go and find a place of your own, now – somewhere that feels right for you. Sit there for awhile, and look, and listen; then come and tell me what you see and hear."

So Pete went into the forest to look for his own secret place. He walked at random, following first one animal track and then another, until presently the ground began to rise gently, and the trees grew smaller, and closer together.

Suddenly a great rock rose out of the forest. Gray lichens grew on it, and it

glistened with water trickling down its face. On the very top trees grew, and between their trunks the dusty sunlight sifted down. In a small mossy clearing at the base of the rock grew a tree with big buttressed roots, spreading out from the trunk like the arms of a chair.

Pete sat down against the trunk and rested his arm on one of the buttresses. It felt right for him. Then he shut his eyes and listened. The air was full of murmurs and crackling, and nearby he smelled the strong, ropy smell of one of the shrubs Barney had shown him. Something – a small bird, was it? – fluttered briefly near his cheek.

When he told Barney about the secret place he had found, the old man nodded. He told Pete that he should go there each day. "It will teach you to care," he said.

So each day Pete went to his secret place. He rested his hand on the trunk of his tree until the rough bark felt warm. He listened, and he looked at the life going on in that small place; and afterwards he sat on the veranda with Barney and told him what he had seen that day.

Barney nodded gently, and once again Pete asked about the spirit of the forest.

"What does it look like, Barney?" he asked.

Barney shrugged. "It is like anything you think of," he said. "It can take many shapes. It may be a bird, or a flower, or a lizard, or even a leaf. You come to learn the signs."

He gave Pete's arm a friendly squeeze. "Don't be in such a hurry. There's plenty of time to see things. You're one of the family now – you sure are." He chuckled. "One day," said Barney, "when I'm old and full of sawdust, you can come and look after us all! Our family, boy – it needs looking after."

The light in the clearing was beginning to fade. In the high treetops there was a small skirmish as birds settled down into their nests; and in the darkening sky the first stars had appeared like pale moths. "Get away home to your nest," said Barney. "There's another day tomorrow."

Pete raced home in the twilight. One day,
he was thinking, when he left school, he'd

save up his money and he'd buy Uncle Alan's farm. And then he'd be able to help Barney look after his forest; and he'd hunt for him, too. He couldn't wait to tell Barney his wonderful plan.

Trouble

The next morning, as Pete was putting on his jacket, he felt a hand on his shoulder. "If I remember rightly, young fella," said Uncle Alan, "we didn't finish that job down at the cattle yards – remember? Shouldn't take a minute."

But like all of Uncle Alan's little jobs, this one grew and grew until lunchtime. And then, after lunch, as he was trying to sneak away for a second time, his aunt appeared in the doorway.

"I want a word with you, Pete." As she spoke she pointed to the calendar hanging on the porch wall. "One week today," she said, "your parents will be coming to fetch you home. And what am I going to tell them about the homework you brought with you? There's no putting it off any longer; you'd better finish it today!"

It was no use arguing. It was clear that she meant what she said. Pete sat down at the kitchen table and stared blankly at the pages. He was worried about Barney.

"He'll be wondering why I didn't come today," he thought. "He'll think I don't care anymore. He might even think I've gone home without bothering to say goodbye." There was nothing for it but to race through his homework so that he could get back to the old man and reassure him.

But Pete was a slow worker at the best of times, and trying to hurry was like being in one of those dreams where you're running and running, yet always on the same spot. Two whole days went by before his aunt and uncle would let him go out again.

Pete didn't want to take any chances. His plan was to slip through the fence behind the house; but to his dismay his uncle was there, re-straining a broken wire. "It's blowing up nor'west again," said Alan, glancing at the sky. "A good day for you and me to burn off that patch where the oats are going in. Shouldn't take a minute."

As usual, one job led to another, but by the middle of the afternoon Pete was free at last. The dusty earth smoked under his boots as he raced toward the river.

When he got to the clearing, he heard coughing coming from the hut. He looked inside and saw Barney lying on his rough bed. His breathing was rapid, and beads of sweat stood on his face.

"Barney!" whispered Pete. But the old man didn't answer. He seemed to be asleep.

Pete ran back to tell his uncle. Alan was changing the oil in his tractor. He frowned as he listened to Pete. "What a time to get sick," he grumbled. "I want to get the barley headed while the nor'wester lasts, and then there's all this grass to cut. Still, I suppose I'll have to go." He threw down the oilcan and set off with Pete for the forest. When they reached the hut, Pete lagged behind his uncle, scared that the old man might have died. It was a relief to see him open his eyes.

"Hi there, Pop!" boomed Uncle Alan. "Couldn't see you for all the cobwebs. Your window's very clean though," he chuckled, punching a fist through the glassless frame. "How are you doing, old soldier?"

"Just a cold," said Barney faintly. "I'll be right as rain."

Uncle Alan pulled a blanket up over the old man. "You sure will!" he said cheerfully. "Keep warm and snug. I'll send Pete back with some of our famous onion soup."

He winked at Pete as he stooped through the doorway. "I don't think that it's anything too serious. The trouble with Barney is that he hasn't any friends here, not even any close family, really. It gets to a guy after awhile." He saw Pete's anxious look and grinned.

"Don't worry, boy, he'll be all right. He's a tough old rooster. Still, I don't think he should be living on his own out there for much longer."

He looked thoughtful. "I might get in touch with that niece of his – Mary or Marie, or whatever her name is. She should at least come to see him. It's not *all* our responsibility."

Pete had heard his aunt say that Barney had a relative who was a nurse. He hoped she would stay to look after him until he was better. "It's only a cold," Pete told himself. "He's going to be as right as rain."

Uncle Alan seemed in a very sociable mood that evening when a neighbor called in. Drowsily, Pete listened to the two men discussing the harvest. But then his heart missed a beat. "What do you think about that piece of forest, Jim?" Uncle Alan was saying. "Could you grow crops there?"

Jim nodded. "No problem, Alan." The two men sat silently for a moment, and then Jim said: "But I thought your hands were tied, with the old man being there."

Uncle Alan leaned across the table. "I'm not taking any bets at this stage," he said confidentially, "but the old guy might be going away. A bit of a vacation, you might say." He sounded pleased at the idea.

That night, Pete tossed in bed, unable to sleep. The nor'west wind was blowing in through the windows, filling the room with a warm fragrance. He could hardly believe that his uncle really meant to cut down the trees. They offered a home to so many other living things, and they were ancient – they'd put down their roots in the land long before human eyes had looked upon it. Their smell was the smell of the earth, and their silence was filled with mystery. To cut them down would be to destroy more than just the trees. And what would happen to Barney?

He lay there imagining the roar of the bulldozer as it bit into the forest. He saw Barney's trees falling over one after the other and the sky rushing in to fill the gaps. He

tried to think of someone who could help
Barney – someone who really cared. But
there was no one.

"If I could do magic," he thought, "I could
hide Barney's forest in a great cloud of mist
when they come to chop it down; or I could
put a shield around it to keep it from harm."

Pete closed his eyes tight and in his mind drew a white circle around the forest. It was a very big circle, including the trees, and the river, and the hawk that wheeled above it, and Barney lying in his ramshackle old hut; and before it was half done, he had fallen asleep.

Pete's Remedy

When he awoke in the morning, a high, unfamiliar voice floated up to him from the kitchen. Barney's niece, Marie, had arrived. He crept to the landing and peered down.

"Where's Uncle, then?" she asked.

"He's still living in the forest," said Pete's aunt. "And he still seems to love that old hut. Pete can take you to see him after breakfast. But you'll need to put on some boots. You won't get far in those light shoes of yours."

After breakfast they set out. Pete strode ahead silently while Marie trudged behind. "How much farther is it?" she wanted to know.

They came to the bridge. She stared at it in horror. "How can I possibly cross that?" she said.

"Walk sideways," said Pete. "Like me." He went back and took her hand, and they shuffled slowly across.

They came to the hut. Marie stared in disbelief at the smoke-blackened clothes hanging from the rafters. Then she stepped gingerly inside, while Pete listened from the veranda.

She peered at the motionless figure on the bed. "Hi, Uncle!" she said brightly. "It's me – Marie! How are you feeling?"

Barney opened his eyes. "I'm all right," he murmured. "Right as rain." He closed his eyes again.

Marie felt his pulse. "You're going to be just fine, Uncle," she said, "but you'd be so much more comfortable in a nice warm place with someone to look after you. Just till you're feeling better. Just a vacation, Uncle."

Barney cleared his throat. "Where's the boy?" he whispered.

Marie sighed. "Will you come home with me?"

"This is my home," said Barney.

Marie patted the old man's head. "Think about it, Uncle," she said. "Please."

She came out of the hut, brushing her skirt. "He can't live in a place like this," she said to Pete. "I can't even see a stove where I could make him a warm drink. He should be in an old people's home where he could be looked after properly. At his age he's entitled to a few comforts, the poor old thing."

Pete glared at her. "Barney doesn't want to go away," he said. "This is his home. He has to stay here to look after the forest."

Marie sighed. "The forest will just have to look after itself, won't it? Things have to change. Now, are you coming back to the house?"

"No, not yet," said Pete, and he turned and ran back into the forest.

When he reached the hut he stood in the doorway, looking down at Barney. The old man appeared to be asleep. An empty sugar bag lay under the bed.

Pete took the sack into the forest and began quickly filling it with all the herbs that Barney had told him were good to use if you were sick: buds of young willow-green, and the inner bark of the tea-tree, gathered from the sunny side of the trunk as Barney had shown him. When the bag was full he took it back to the hut.

"Barney," he whispered, "I've brought some medicine, and I'm going to set a fire in

the grate." Barney's eyes were open, but he made no sign.

"I'm putting the sack by your bed," said Pete, "and there's firewood on the veranda."

Barney's eyes followed Pete's movements, but still he said nothing. Pete tiptoed out. He stood on the veranda, blinking in the sunlight. It was very still. Bees hummed in the shadows, and there was a warm smell of spice in the air. Never had the forest seemed so beautiful, and so frail. One puff, and it could all blow away like thistledown. He wished that he could capture it, in some way, like a landscape in a magic mirror.

"My secret place," said Pete suddenly. He entered the forest,

following secret paths until he came to his mossy clearing. He sat down under his tree, fitting himself snugly between its buttresses. Above him rose the rock, a dark core of stone older by far than the surrounding trees.

He shut his eyes. At once a picture of the rock began to form in his mind, a shadowy shape braided with glistening threads of light. He held the shape with his inner eye, and whispered, "Barney is sick and needs help. I have given him some plants to make him better, but I am afraid that someone will come to take him away before he is well. And then there will be no one to look after the forest. The bulldozers will come and fell the trees, and turn the river into a ditch, and the fish will die, and the birds, too, and the insects. Please, help Barney."

The shape of the rock in his mind had grown in clarity until he could see the lichen clinging to its silver surface, and the young ferns sprouting from the crevices where the water trickled down.

And suddenly it seemed to Pete that he was standing on top of the rock, looking down on the ancient forest and the farmland stretching away beyond.

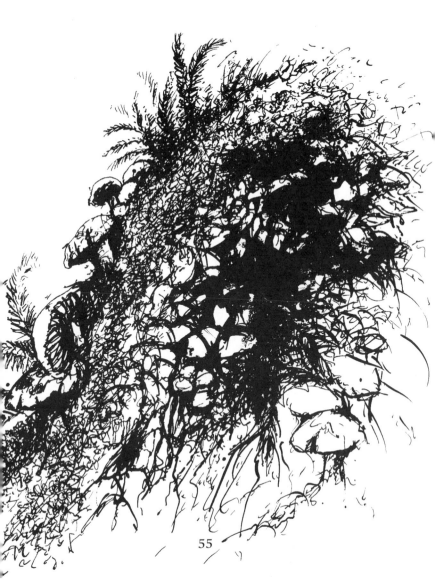

Far below, the
river encircled the
forest like an island.
It flowed around and
around, a flashing circle of
light, then darkening quickly to a
murky-brown color, and moving
faster. It made him giddy to look at it. A
sudden cold breath rippled off the water,
and Pete shivered. He opened his eyes.

"Have I been awake or asleep?" he asked
himself. Above the great rock, a hawk was
climbing into a darkening sky. It rose in
slowly-widening circles, like ripples in a pool
of air. A shadow passed over the clearing,
and there was an unmistakable rumble of

distant thunder. Pete jumped to his feet and ran.

As he burst out of the forest, the long grass crackled, and a cold wind whipped his legs. To the south, a solitary tree behind the farmhouse gleamed ashen-white before the advancing storm cloud. Pete was racing in big leaps, reaching the back porch just as the first icy drops began to fall.

Moments later, he stood with his forehead pressed to the window, watching a squall of rain drive across the land, and the forest vanishing behind it.

The Promise

Uncle Alan came roaring through the gate on his tractor. He stood at the wheel like a charioteer, water dripping from his face. "You wouldn't read about it!" he grumbled, as he kicked off his boots in the porch. "I never saw a storm come up so quick. Half an hour ago there wasn't a cloud in the sky."

But Pete, with his nose still pressed to the window, was elated.

"Flood, river, flood!" he whispered. "Then nobody can take Barney away."

But as the rain continued to rumble on the roof all through the afternoon and into the early evening, he began to feel anxious. What if the rain kept on and on, and Barney was swept away?

He imagined the hut swirling down the river like a sodden sparrow's nest, and shivered. If anything happened to the old man, it would be his fault. "I made the bad weather come," he said to himself, "by calling to the spirit for help." And now the rain didn't seem to know when to stop.

"Do you think it will be still raining tomorrow?" he asked his uncle.

Alan shook his head. "I wouldn't know," he said. "We often get storms at this time of year, but this one looks like being a bad one. I've never seen the river come up as fast as it has this time. It wouldn't surprise me if the bridge gets washed away!"

By morning the rain had eased to a light drizzle. When Pete looked out of his bedroom window, he discovered that overnight a lake had miraculously appeared. Beyond, the forest was afloat in mist, unreachable as a forest in a dream.

Marie was carrying her suitcase to the car. "I took two days off to come down here," she said. "I'm sorry, but I can't stay any longer."

"Don't worry," said Uncle Alan cheerfully. "If he's still ill, we'll fetch him over somehow, even if we have to hire a rowing boat."

By afternoon, the water had gone down sufficiently for Uncle Alan to wade across the fields

in boots. He put on the heavy waders that he used in the winter, and set out to check the fences. Pete went with him, and his uncle piggybacked him over the bad patches.

"The fences seem to be in order," said Alan as they approached the forest, "but I guess the bad news is still to come." And sure enough, when they reached the ridge and looked down, they saw that the bridge had been washed away.

A brown, frothing torrent swirled from bank to bank. A few flax plants rose above the waterline, and on the other side Pete could see a rivulet flowing into the forest where the track had been.

"There's no way of getting the old guy out today," Pete's uncle said, "unless we bring in a helicopter or something. To tell the truth, I'm not sure what to do."

But Pete wasn't listening. He had sensed a movement, a stirring of the leaves; and there, like part of the forest itself, was Barney.

He stood at the edge of the dripping trees, knee-deep in water. His thick trousers, tied at the waist with string, seemed to sag a little more than usual, but otherwise he looked as good as ever.

A frown passed quickly across Uncle Alan's face. "You could have fooled me," he muttered. He cupped his hands. "How are you, old-timer?" Barney's soft reply carried clearly to Pete across the roaring water.

"What's he say?" asked Uncle Alan.

"He says he's right as rain," said Pete.

It was Pete's turn to cup his hands. "Did you find the sack?" he shouted.

Barney's voice floated soft and clear as a whisper in Pete's ear. "I thought you'd gone, boy, without a goodbye to old Barney."

"But I left a sack for you," Pete called back, "full of herbs and things to make you better. Did you find them?"

Barney nodded. "I thought I saw you sitting beside me with a gift in your hand. It

was so clear, I woke up and thought: now where's that sack I saw in my dream? Then I felt around on the floor, and found it. And when I touched it my old numb fingers began to tingle, like when I put my hands on a tree – you know what I'm saying? And I was feeling strong enough to get up, so I brewed some herb tea. I'm right as rain, boy."

Uncle Alan was staring blankly across the river. "What was all that about?" he said grumpily. "I couldn't understand a word."

"He says he's right as rain," said Pete.

"He said that before," said Alan. He shook his head. "Tough old rooster." He began to move along the ridge, checking the fence.

Pete cupped his hands again. "I have to go home tomorrow," he called. Barney nodded.

"But I'll come back in the summer vacation. Are you really all right?"

Barney cleared his throat. "I told you, boy – I'm right as rain."

Uncle Alan had returned. "Come on," he said. "I've got work to do."

Pete turned to wave to Barney. But the old man had gone.

"Uncle Alan," said Pete, as they set off for home, "would you really cut Barney's forest down?"

His uncle gave him a playful jab in the shoulder. "Sure I would. One day, I'll have that place as smooth as a billiard table."

They waded on toward the farm. The water squelched in Pete's boots as he splashed through the shallows.

"But it looks as though I'll have to wait awhile yet," his uncle added.

Yes. Pete knew that, because of his uncle's promise, Barney would be safe so long as he kept well and wanted to stay in his forest home. Not even Barney's niece could change that, he hoped.

But Pete felt as though *he'd* made a promise, too – to Barney and the forest. He'd have to make his parents understand. He'd have to come back and make his aunt and uncle understand. Pete thought about how the old man's hands had tingled when he

touched the sack of herbs beside his bed. It made him feel that he *could* find a way.

Plans were already forming in Pete's mind as he threw off his boots on the porch and ran upstairs to pack.

"Keep strong, Barney!" he whispered to himself. "Keep strong till I get back to you."

TITLES IN THE SERIES

SET 9A

Television Drama
Time for Sale
The Shady Deal
The Loch Ness Monster Mystery
Secrets of the Desert

SET 9B

To JJ From CC
Pandora's Box
The Birthday Disaster
The Song of the Mantis
Helping the Hoiho

SET 9C

Glumly
Rupert and the Griffin
The Tree, the Trunk, and the Tuba
Errol the Peril
Cassidy's Magic

SET 9D

Barney
Get a Grip, Pip!
Casey's Case
Dear Future
Strange Meetings

SET 10A

A Battle of Words
The Rainbow Solution
Fortune's Friend
Eureka
It's a Frog's Life

SET 10B

The Cat Burglar of Pethaven Drive
The Matchbox
In Search of the Great Bears
Many Happy Returns
Spider Relatives

SET 10C

Horrible Hank
Brian's Brilliant Career
Fernitickles
It's All in Your Mind,
    James Robert
Wing High, Gooftah

SET 10D

The Week of the Jellyhoppers
Timothy Whuffenpuffen-
    Whippersnapper
Timedetectors
Ryan's Dog Ringo
The Secret of Kiribu Tapu Lagoon